M.A. Fanton

Tables of Roman Law

SALZWASSER
VERLAG

M.A. Fanton

Tables of Roman Law

1st Edition | ISBN: 978-3-75250-416-3

Place of Publication: Frankfurt am Main, Germany

Year of Publication: 2020

Salzwasser Verlag GmbH, Germany.

Reprint of the original, first published in 1869.

TO

JOSEPH SHARPE, ESQ., LL.D.

READER ON JURISPRUDENCE, CIVIL AND INTERNATIONAL LAW, TO THE FOUR INNS OF COURT,

𝕿𝖍𝖊 𝖋𝖔𝖑𝖑𝖔𝖜𝖎𝖓𝖌 𝕿𝖆𝖇𝖑𝖊𝖘

ARE, BY KIND PERMISSION, RESPECTFULLY DEDICATED.

TABLES OF ROMAN LAW.

BY

M. A. FANTON,

DOCTEUR EN DROIT.

TRANSLATED AND EDITED

BY

C. W. LAW, OF THE MIDDLE TEMPLE, ESQ.,

LONDON:

WYMAN & SONS, 74-75, GREAT QUEEN STREET,

LINCOLN'S-INN FIELDS, W.C.

1869.

THE INSTITUTES OF JUSTINIAN

are divided into Four Books :—

THE FIRST gives some general notions respecting the meaning of the words JUSTITIA and JUS, and then proceeds to treat of PERSONS.

THE SECOND treats of THINGS, of the MEANS OF ACQUIRING PARTICULAR OBJECTS, of SUCCESSIONS TO DECEASED PERSONS, of LEGACIES, and of TRUSTS, or Fidei commissa.

THE THIRD deals with the INHERITANCES OF INTESTATES and other UNIVERSAL INHERITANCES. It also treats of OBLIGATIONS which arise either ex contractu or quasi ex contractu.

THE FOURTH deals with OBLIGATIONS which arise ex delicto or quasi ex delicto ; and with ACTIONS.

It may be seen from the above division that, according to Roman Jurisprudence, the laws of Rome related :—

1. TO PERSONS. 2. TO THINGS. 3. TO ACTIONS.

The Jurists charged with the composition of the Institutes were TRIBONIAN, THEOPHILUS, and DOROTHEUS.

The Four Books of the Institutes are preceded by a Procemium, which serves as an Introduction, and which terminates with the following words :—"D. CP. XI calend. Decembris. D. Justiniano. PP. A. III. Cons."—(Given at Constantinople, on the eleventh day of the Calends of December, in the third consulate of the Emperor Justinian, ever August).

Explanation of the signs employed in these Tables :—

O.L.	...	...	... Older Law.	J.L.	...	...	... Justinian's Law.
B.L.	...	...	... Byzantine Law.	N.	...	...	... Novellæ.

BOOK I.—TABLE I.

Tɪᴛ. I.—De Justitia et Jure.   Tɪᴛ. II.—De Jure naturali, gentium et civili.

" *Jus*, the Law ; *Justitia*, the wish to observe the Jus ; *Jurisprudentia*, the knowledge of the Jus."

LAW (Jus) is divided into :—

1. PUBLIC. (Quod ad statum rei Romanæ spectat.) quod consistit { In Sacris ...... / In Sacerdotibus / In Magistratibus } Dig. I. i. de Just. et Jure.

N.B. The Roman Public Law is only mentioned here, as in the Institutes of Gaius, for memory's sake.

2. PRIVATE

1. NATURAL LAW. (Quod natura omnia animalia docuit.)
1. Union of Male and Female ....
2. Procreation and bringing up of Children ....
3. Legitimate self-defence ....
Common to men as well as to all animals.

2. THE LAW OF NATIONS. (Quod naturalis ratio inter omnes homines constituit.)
1. Slavery by captivity.
2. Nearly all Contracts, with the exception of a few, such as Stipulation, which arises from the Civil Law.
3. The Rights of Property.

N.B. Many commentators divide the Jus Gentium into Primary and Secondary law. The Primary law comprises such principles as arise from the very nature of man. The Secondary law owes its origin to the wants of social life, — usu exigente et humanis necessitatibus.

3. CIVIL LAW. (Quod quisque populus ipse sibi jus constituit.) The Civil Law is either written or unwritten, —aut ex scripto, aut non ex scripto.

1. Wʀɪᴛᴛᴇɴ,—which results from an express declaration of the Legislative will.

1. Lᴀᴡs.—A law is that which was enacted by the whole Roman people on its being proposed by a senatorian magistrate, as a consul. It was binding on all the people.

2. Pʟᴇʙɪsᴄɪᴛᴀ.—A plebiscitum is that which was enacted in the comitia by the plebs on its being proposed by a plebeian magistrate, as a tribune. (The Lex Hortensia gives plebiscita the force of laws.)

3. Sᴇɴᴀᴛᴜs-Cᴏɴsᴜʟᴛᴀ.—A senatus-consultum is that which the Senate commands or appoints.

4. Iᴍᴘᴇʀɪᴀʟ Cᴏɴsᴛɪᴛᴜᴛɪᴏɴs.
1. *Rescripta.*—Answers given by the Emperor to magistrates who requested his assistance in the decision of doubtful points (per epistolam constituit).
2. *Decreta.*—Judicial sentences given by the Emperor (cognoscens decrevit).
3. *Edicta.*—General laws spontaneously promulgated by the Emperor, the Rescripta and Decreta being ordinarily personal.

5. Mᴀɢɪsᴛᴇʀɪᴀʟ Eᴅɪᴄᴛs. Rules or declarations of the magistrates on their entering into office, by which they made known the principles by which they intended to be guided during their administration. This right of publishing edicts belongs to the ....
1. Prætors.. { Edictum annuum .. Given by the Prætors on entering upon their office. / „ perpetuum.. Ed. of Salvius Julianus. / Edictum repentinum.
2. Curule Ediles.
3. Governors or Presidents in the Provinces who fulfilled the functions of Prætors.

6. Rᴇsᴘᴏɴsᴀ Pʀᴜᴅᴇɴᴛᴜᴍ. Decisions and advice of the Jurists, whom the Emperors had authorized to settle the law.
The Emperor Augustus was the first to allow certain jurists the privilege of being authorities with regard to the settling of the law.
The Emperor Adrian decided that when the jurists were all of the same opinion their decisions should have the force of law.
In Justinian's reign the Responsa Prudentum form the basis of all Roman legislation. (Digest.)

2. Cᴜsᴛᴏᴍᴀʀʏ or Uɴᴡʀɪᴛᴛᴇɴ Law (quod usus comprobavit). The principal thing established by the unwritten law was the prohibition of gifts between husband and wife.

3

BOOK I.—TABLE II.

Tɪᴛ. III.—De Jure Personarum.   Tɪᴛ. IV.—De Ingenuis.   Tɪᴛ. V.—De Libertinis.
Tɪᴛ. VI.—Qui quibus ex causis manumittere non possunt.
Tɪᴛ. VII.—De Lege Fusia Caninia sublata.

"Persons may be divided either into *Liberi* and *Servi*, or into persons *Sui Juris* and persons *Alieni Juris*."

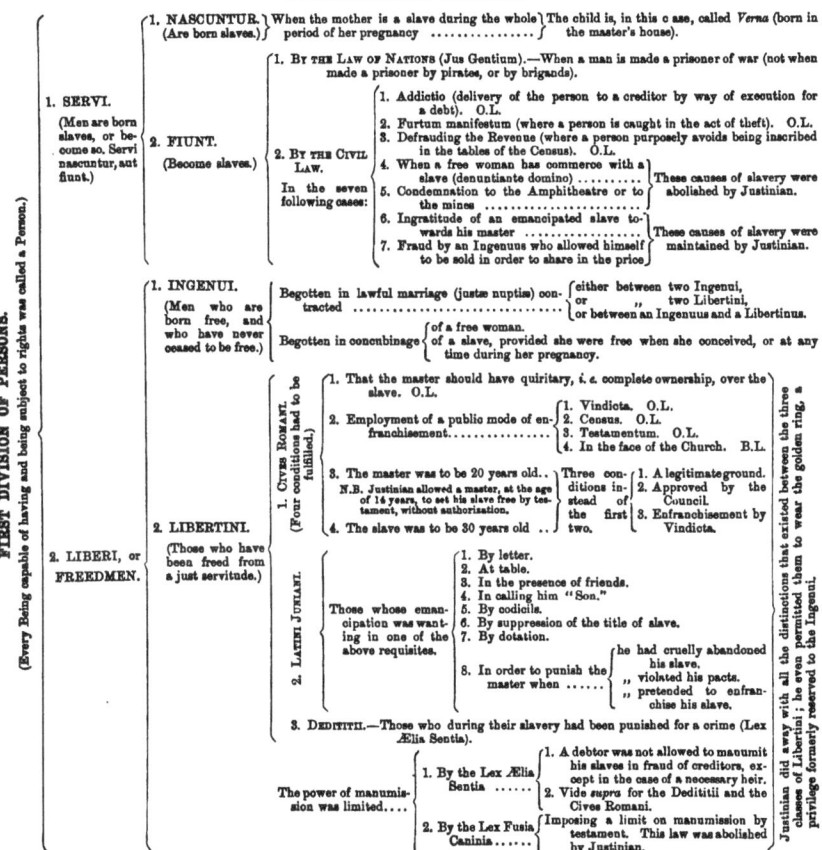

BOOK I.—TABLE III.

Tit. VIII.—De iis qui sui vel alieni juris sunt.   Tit. IX.—De Patria Potestate.   Tit. X.—De Nuptiis.

Tit. XI.—De Adoptionibus.   Tit. XII.—Quibus modis Jus Potestatis solvitur.

SECOND DIVISION OF PERSONS into—

1. ALIENI JURIS.

1. SONS, and those Persons under the Paternal power.

1. Children begotten in lawful marriage, for which three requisites, viz. :

  1. Puberty (14), Nubility (12).

  2. Consent { 1. Of the parties. 2. Of the heads of their families.

  3. Connubium, which could not exist in seven cases, viz. :
- 1. Where the quality of citizen was wanting.
- 2. Where the parties were within the prohibited degrees of relationship (agnati as well as cognati).
- 3. Where one of the parties was tutor to the other, or governor of the province in which the other party was living.
- 4. Former marriage not dissolved.
- 5. Where there existed certain differences of rank.
- 6. Between an adulterer and his accomplice, or between a ravisher and the woman he had violated.
- 7. Between a Jew and a Christian.

A lawful marriage was determined by, either,
- 1. The death of one of the parties.
- 2. The loss of liberty and of citizenship.
- 3. Captivity.
- 4. Divorce.

2. Children begotten in a marriage in which the connubium was wanting.

A lawful marriage differed from :
- 1. *Concubinatus*, which did not confer the title of wife on the woman. The children were sui juris, and deprived of all family rights.
- 2. *Stuprum*, or temporary union of the sexes, whence are born the "spurii," or "vulgo concepti."
- 3. *Contubernium*, or union of slaves. The children were subject to the laws of agnation, which on their enfranchisement produced the same hindrances to a lawful marriage as the law of cognation.(a)

(a) Relationship, according to the Roman law, was of two kinds :
- 1. *Cognation*, or natural relationship.
- 2. *Agnation*, or relationship by the civil law.

3. Natural children legitimated.—This might be done :
- 1. By the father's subsequent marriage with the child's mother.
- 2. By oblation to the Curia.
- 3. By rescript of the Emperor. Nov. 74 and 89.

4. Adopted children (alieni juris).—Adoption.

1. Modes of Adoption.
- 1. Before Justinian's time three things necessary :
  - 1. Mancipation of the child to the person adopting him.
  - 2. Remancipation of the child to his father.
  - 3. The fictitious process of law called in Jure Cessio, by which the father gave up the child to the adopting parent.
- 2. Under Justinian : Declarations before the Prætor, made respectively by the parties interested.

2. Effects of Adoption.
- 1. Before Justinian's time.—Patria potestas and its consequences.
- 2. In Justinian's time.—Patria potestas only in the case of the adopting party being an ascendant. If he were a stranger, adoption gave right of succession ab intestato.

5. Arrogated children (sui juris).—Arrogation.

1. Modes of Arrogation :
- 1. Before Justinian's time.—By the law of the people.
- 2. In Justinian's time.—By a rescript.

2. Effects of Arrogation :
- 1. Before Justinian's time.—Absolute power over the arrogated person, his children, and his property.
- 2. In Justinian's time.—The power over his property was reduced to the usufruct thereof.

Note. The Libertinus could only be adopted by his patron. If the master of a slave declared that he adopted him, this declaration only amounted to a simple enfranchisement.

2. WOMEN, in Manu Mariti
- 1. By confarreatio.
- 2. By coemptio.
- 3. By Usus (usucapio annalis, uninterrupted by the trinoctium).

3. FREEMEN, in Mancipio ...
- 1. Addiction of insolvent debtors to their creditors. O.L.
- 2. Mancipation of children by the father.

4. SLAVES (*vide* Table II.)

2. SUI JURIS.

1. Who have neither tutor nor curator.—These persons may be kinds of them. And can still from the time of their birth, for this it will suffice that they should belong to no other family than their own, even to the Paterfamilias's power over those who composed his family was so fictitious.

1. According to the ancient law, he was considered as the owner both of his children and of his slaves; and he exercised this power over his children :
- 1. The right of life and death.
- 2. The right of selling them.
- 3. The right of exposing them.
- 4. The right of delivering them up by way of reparation for wrongs they had caused.
- 5. The right of killing them, if born deformed.
- 6. Finally, everything the child had belonged to his father.

2. During the Republic, this absolute power was maintained in nearly all its severity, though the Paterfamilias was already beginning to be looked upon as the sovereign chief, instead of the owner of his family.

3. The Pater Familias— Might exercise two kinds of power, which were restricted by the Emperors.

1. Patria Potestas. In Justinian's time :
- 1. As regards persons.
  - 1. The father can no longer sell his children, excepting at the time of their birth (sanguinolenti), and in cases of extreme poverty.
  - 2. He has no longer the power of life and death over them.
  - 3. He can no longer expose them.
  - 4. He must apply to the magistrate if he wish to inflict an extraordinary punishment on them.
- 2. As regards property. The son may enjoy a peculium.

2. Dominica Potestas— Formerly absolute, was limited by degrees, until Justinian's time, when :
- 1. As regards persons.
  - 1. The master is prohibited from punishing his slaves too severely.
  - 2. The master might be compelled to sell his slaves upon equitable terms (expedit enim reipublicæ ne sua re quis male utatur).
- 2. As regards things. The older law, "that everything the slave had should belong to the master, but that the slave might enjoy a peculium," was maintained.

As to determination of the Dominica Potestas, vide Table II.

4. The Paternal Power— Might be determined :
- 1. By the natural death of the father of the family.
- 2. By arrogation.
- 3. By emancipation ....
- 4. By the natural death of the filiusfamilias.
  - 1. Old form.
  - 2. Anastasian's system.
  - 3. Justinian's mode.
- 5. By the child's attaining certain dignities ...
  - 1. That of the Patriciate. J.L.
  - 2. That of Consul. N.
  - 3. That of Vestal. O.L.
  - 4. That of Flamen dialis. O.L.
  - 5. That of Prætor or Præses.
  - 6. That of Bishop, &c.
- 6. By the major or media capitis deminutio of the father.
- 7. By the major, media, or minima capitis deminutio of the son.

2. Under Tutors.
3. Under Curators. } (*Vide* Table IV.)

BOOK I.—TABLE IV.

Tit. XIII.—De Tutelis.   Tit. XIV.—Qui Testamento Tutores dari possunt.   Tit. XV.—De Legitima Adgnatorum Tutela.
Tit. XVI.—De Capitis Deminutione.   Tit. XVII.—De Legitima Patronorum Tutela.
Tit. XVIII.—De Legitima Parentium Tutela.   Tit. XIX.—De Fiduciaria Tutela.
Tit. XX.—De Atiliano Tutore et eo qui ex Lege Julia et Titia dabitur.   Tit. XXI.—De Auctoritate Tutorum.
Tit. XXII.—Quibus modis Tutela finitur.   Tit. XXIII.—De Curationibus.
Tit. XXIV.—De Satisdatione Tutorum vel Curatorum.   Tit. XXV.—De Excusationibus Tutorum vel Curatorum.
Tit. XXVI.—De suspectis Tutoribus vel Curatoribus.

SECOND DIVISION OF PERSONS.

1. ALIENI JURIS (vide Table III.).

1. WHO HAVE NEITHER TUTOR NOR CURATOR (personæ quæ neutro jure tenentur).

"Tutela est vis ac potestas in capite libero, ad tuendum eum qui propter ætatem se defendere nequit, jure civili data ac permissa." There are two distinct periods in the tutelage:—1. Until the child has entered on his eighth year; until then the tutor represents the child, and manages its affairs. 2. From the beginning of the eighth year until the age of puberty, during which time the child may better its condition, but is not allowed to make it worse. The child must obtain the tutor's sanction. The tutor supplies what is wanting to complete the pupil's legal character. *Note.*—This Table must be read horizontally and vertically.

2. SUI JURIS. — UNDER A TUTOR.

The different kinds of Tutelage.	Of those who may be under a Tutor.	Of those persons who may be Tutors.	When and how the different kinds of tutelage were instituted.	When and how, beyond the common causes of condition accomplished and time expired, tutelage may be determined.	
1. Testamentary Tutelage.	Legitimate children who have become "sui juris" without "capitis deminutio."	Testamentary tutors are those with whom there is "testamenti factio," and who are capable of holding a public office.	Testamentary tutelage was instituted when the paterfamilias had appointed, by testament, one or more tutors for such of his children as remained under his power and had not attained the age of puberty.	**Of the Pupil.** 1. By natural death. 2. By major capitis deminutio. 3. By media cap. dem. 4. By minima cap. dem. 5. Conventio in manum. 6. Puberty (14), Nubility (12).	**Of the Tutor.** 1. By natural death. 2. By major capitis deminutio, or loss of liberty. 3. By media cap. dem., or loss of rights of civisenship. 4. By minima cap.dem., or loss of family rights. (This only applies to the legal tutelage of the Agnati.) 5. Excuse. 6. Destitution. 7. Remarriage of the mother or grandmother tutoress.—J.L.
2. Testamentary Tutelage confirmed.	Legitimate children who have become "sui juris" by emancipation.	In the case of testament'ry tutelage confirmed, the appointment must be confirmed by the magistrate. The following may be testamentary tutors, or confirmed testamentary tutors. 1. A Paterfamilias. 2. A Filiusfamilias. 3. A Slave (if his liberty were given at the same time). Since Justinian, a slave was freed by the simple fact of his being made tutor. 4. The slave of another when he shall be made free." 5. A madman, or person under the age of 25 years, —on his becoming of sound mind, or on his attaining his majority.	As regards the confirmed testamentary tutelage, the magistrate confirmed the testament of the father who appointed a tutor to his emancipated son.		

3. LEGAL TUTELAGE.

1. Of the Agnati.	Filiifamilias who have become "sui juris" without "capitis deminutio."	The nearest Agnati	According to the law of the Twelve Tables, the tutelage was conferred on the Agnati when the Paterfamilias died intestate with regard to the nomination of a tutor. It was also conferred on the Agnati when the testamentary tutor was dead.		
2. Of Patrons.	Libertini	Patrons, or their heirs, if the latter be not incapacitated from holding such a charge, as in the case of women or a minor of 25 years.	As those Libertini who had not attained the age of puberty had a tutor, they could only be legal tutelage of the patron.		
3. Of Ascendants.	Emancipated Filiifamilias who have not attained the age of puberty.	The Paterfamilias who emancipated the child under the age of puberty.	The emancipator had rights similar to those of the patron.		
4. Fiduciary Tutelage.	Emancipated Filiifamilias who have not attained the age of puberty.	The other male children who have attained the majority of 25 years, and who were under the power of the emancipator before his death.	Fiduciary tutelage is but a sort of legal tutelage.	**EXCUSES COMMON TO TUTORS AND TO CURATORS.** N.B.—Tutelage and Curatorship were public charges, which could not be avoided without giving a valid excuse.	
5. Dative Tutelage.	1. Legitimate children who have become "sui juris" without "capitis deminutio." 2. Legitimate children who have become "sui juris" by emancipation. 3. Natural children begotten in concubinage. 4. Natural children "spurii or vulgo concepti." 5. Libertini.	At Rome, dative tutors (tutores dativi) were those appointed by the "Prætor urbanus," and by a majority of the tribunes of the plebs (Lex Atilia). *In the provinces* they were appointed by the "Presides" under the "leges Julia et Titia." At a later period (under Claudius) they were named by the Consuls. This power was transferred by Antoninus Pius to the "Prætors," but with inquiry. Under Justinian, dative tutors were those who were appointed by the special city magistrates, in those cases in which the pupil's fortune did not exceed 500 "solidi."	("tutor dativus" was appointed in three cases:) 1. When there was no testamentary or no legal tutor. 2. When the testamentary tutor could not enter upon his charge until the happening of a certain event. 3. When the testamentary tutor excused himself from the burden of the tutelage, or when he had been removed on suspicion.	1. The number of children living, or killed in battle. 2. Administration of the fiscal department. 3. Persons absent on the service of the State. 4. When invested with magisterial power.	At Rome,—Three. In Italy.—Four. The provinces.—Five. The Exchequer and the Treasury are united under the Emperors. Perpetual excuse during the absence and for the subsequent year. Temporary with regard to those tutelages and curatorships with which they were charged before their absence. This only forms a valid excuse for future tutelages or curatorships.
6. Optive Tutelage.				5. Lawsuit (with the pupil or adult) embracing the whole of the property, or suit for an inheritance. 6. Three tutelages or curatorships, if unsolicited; or even one tutelage or curatorship, if it be a very complicated one. 7. Poverty. 8. Illness. Temporary excuse. 9. Ignorance, if the person be incapable of administering. 10. When the tutor or curator is named through enmity. 11. Deadly enmity against the father of the pupil or adult, if no reconciliation has taken place. 12. Being seventy years of age. 13. Being a military person. 14. The exercise of a liberal profession at Rome.	

Of Curators and of those under Curators.—Persons under 25 years of age can on that ground alone receive a curator, but they are not obliged to do so excepting in the three following cases, in which the adversary, the debtor, or the tutor, are obliged to ask for a curator, if they wish to insure the validity of their suit, of their payment, or of their accounts, viz. :—1. In lawsuits ; 2. When a debtor wishes to discharge a debt he owes to the adolescent; 3. When the tutor wishes to settle his accounts with him. Curators may therefore (therein differing from tutors) be given "ad certam causam."

4. UNDER A CURATOR.

Different kinds of Curatorship.	Of those who may be under a Curator.	Of those persons who may be Curators.	When and how Curatorships may be determined.
1. Testamentary Curatorship confirmed	Madmen and prodigals within the meaning of the Prætorian law. Madmen and prodigals within the meaning of the law of the Twelve Tables.	All those who have no good excuse to offer against their nomination, and who have not been put aside as "suspected."	
2. Legal Curatorship of the Agnati	1. The two classes above cited. 2. The deaf, the dumb, and the blind.	Curators, as well as tutors, are obliged to find security (" satisdatio ") excepting :—	
3. Dative Curatorship	3. Those under 25 years of age, when the curatorship is obligatory.	1. Testamentary curators and confirmed testamentary curators. 2. Where they have been appointed upon inquiry.	All curatorships end with the causes that led to their establishment.
4. Curatorship "Ventris nomine"			
5. " " " ex Carboniano edicto"	The names of these different kinds of curatorship explain sufficiently to whom they are applied.	Tutors and curators may be removed as suspected when they do not faithfully manage the property, or when they are men of bad conduct.	
6. " " " Bonorum absentis "			
7. " " " Bonorum debitoris, qui solvendo non est "			
8. " " " Hereditatis jacentis "			
9. There were also some curatorships concurrent with tutorships	slaves		

BOOK II.—TABLE V.

Tit. I.—De Divisione Rerum et Qualitate.   Tit. II.—De Rebus Corporalibus et Incorporalibus.

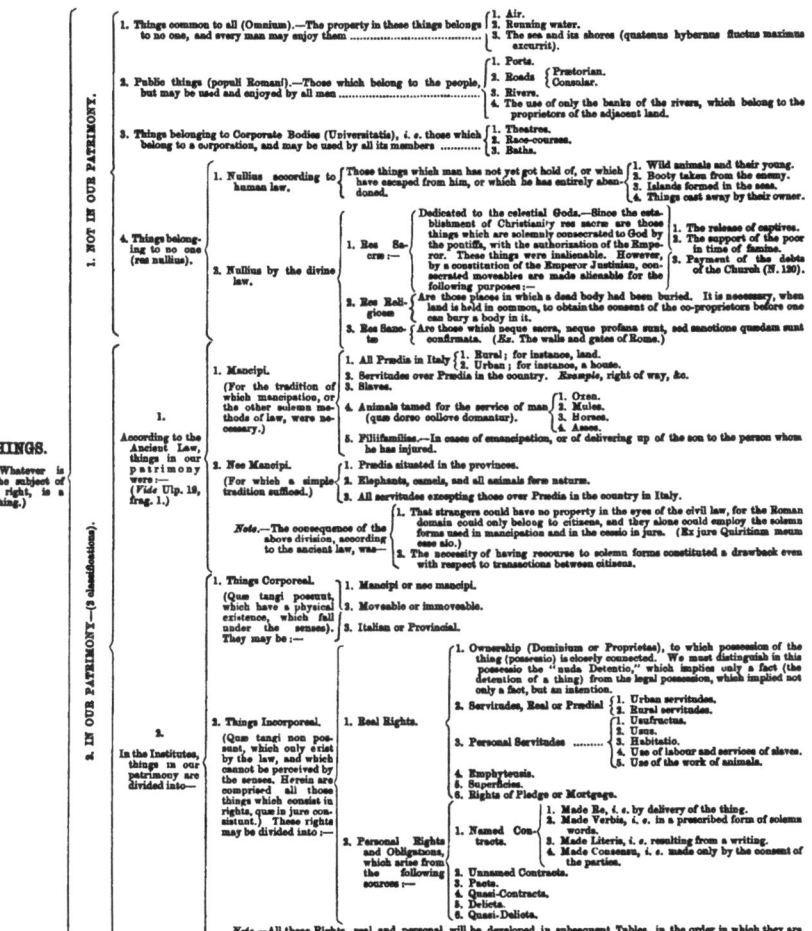

THINGS.
(Whatever is the subject of a right, is a thing.)

1. NOT IN OUR PATRIMONY.

1. Things common to all (Omnium).—The property in these things belongs to no one, and every man may enjoy them ....
  1. Air.
  2. Running water.
  3. The sea and its shores (quatenus hybernus fluctus maximus excurrit).

2. Public things (populi Romani).—Those which belong to the people, but may be used and enjoyed by all men ....
  1. Ports.
  2. Roads { Prætorian. Consular.
  3. Rivers.
  4. The use of only the banks of the rivers, which belong to the proprietors of the adjacent land.

3. Things belonging to Corporate Bodies (Universitatis), i. e. those which belong to a corporation, and may be used by all its members ....
  1. Theatres.
  2. Race-courses.
  3. Baths.

4. Things belonging to no one (res nullius).

  1. Nullius according to human law.
Those things which man has not yet got hold of, or which have escaped from him, or which he has entirely abandoned.
    1. Wild animals and their young.
    2. Booty taken from the enemy.
    3. Islands formed in the seas.
    4. Things cast away by their owner.

  2. Nullius by the divine law.
    1. Res Sacræ :—
Dedicated to the celestial Gods.—Since the establishment of Christianity res sacræ are those things which are solemnly consecrated to God by the pontiffs, with the authorization of the Emperor. These things were inalienable. However, by a constitution of the Emperor Justinian, consecrated moveables are made alienable for the following purposes :—
      1. The release of captives.
      2. The support of the poor in time of famine.
      3. Payment of the debts of the Church (N. 120).

    2. Res Religiosæ
Are those places in which a dead body had been buried. It is necessary, when land is held in common, to obtain the consent of the co-proprietors before one can bury a body in it.

    3. Res Sanctæ
Are those which neque sacra, neque profana sunt, sed sanctione quædam sunt confirmata. (Ex. The walls and gates of Rome.)

2. IN OUR PATRIMONY—(2 classifications).

1. According to the Ancient Law, things in our patrimony were :— (Vide Ulp. 19, frag. 1.)

  1. Mancipi. (For the tradition of which mancipation, or the other solemn methods of law, were necessary.)
    1. All Prædia in Italy { 1. Rural ; for instance, land. 2. Urban ; for instance, a house.
    2. Servitudes over Prædia in the country. Example, right of way, &c.
    3. Slaves.
    4. Animals tamed for the service of man (quæ dorso collove domantur).
      1. Oxen. 2. Mules. 3. Horses. 4. Asses.
    5. Filiifamilias.—In cases of emancipation, or of delivering up of the son to the person whom he has injured.

  2. Nec Mancipi. (For which a simple tradition sufficed.)
    1. Prædia situated in the provinces.
    2. Elephants, camels, and all animals feræ naturæ.
    3. All servitudes excepting those over Prædia in the country in Italy.

  Note.—The consequence of the above division, according to the ancient law, was—
    1. That strangers could have no property in the eyes of the civil law, for the Roman domain could only belong to citizens, and they alone could employ the solemn forms used in mancipation and in the cessio in jure. (Ex jure Quiritium meum esse aio.)
    2. The necessity of having recourse to solemn forms constituted a drawback even with respect to transactions between citizens.

2. In the Institutes, things in our patrimony are divided into—

  1. Things Corporeal. (Quæ tangi possunt, which have a physical existence, which fall under the senses.) They may be :—
    1. Mancipi or nec mancipi.
    2. Moveable or immoveable.
    3. Italian or Provincial.

  2. Things Incorporeal. (Quæ tangi non possunt, which only exist by the law, and which cannot be perceived by the senses. Herein are comprised all those things which consist in rights, quæ in jure consistunt.) These rights may be divided into :—

    1. Real Rights.
      1. Ownership (Dominium or Proprietas), to which possession of the thing (possessio) is closely connected. We must distinguish in this possessio the "nuda Detentio," which implies only a fact (the detention of a thing) from the legal possession, which implied not only a fact, but an intention.
      2. Servitudes, Real or Prædial { 1. Urban servitudes. 2. Rural servitudes.
      3. Personal Servitudes .... { 1. Usufructus. 2. Usus. 3. Habitatio. 4. Use of labour and services of slaves. 5. Use of the work of animals.
      4. Emphyteusis.
      5. Superficies.
      6. Rights of Pledge or Mortgage.

    2. Personal Rights and Obligations, which arise from the following sources :—
      1. Named Contracts.
        1. Made Re, i. e. by delivery of the thing.
        2. Made Verbis, i. e. in a prescribed form of solemn words.
        3. Made Literis, i. e. resulting from a writing.
        4. Made Consensu, i. e. made only by the consent of the parties.
      2. Unnamed Contracts.
      3. Pacts.
      4. Quasi-Contracts.
      5. Delicta.
      6. Quasi-Delicta.

Note.—All these Rights, real and personal, will be developed in subsequent Tables, in the order in which they are treated in the Institutes.

BOOK II.—TABLE VI.

Vide Table V. Tit. I.—De Divisione Rerum et Qualitate.   Tit. VI.—De Usucapionibus et longi Temporis Possessionibus.

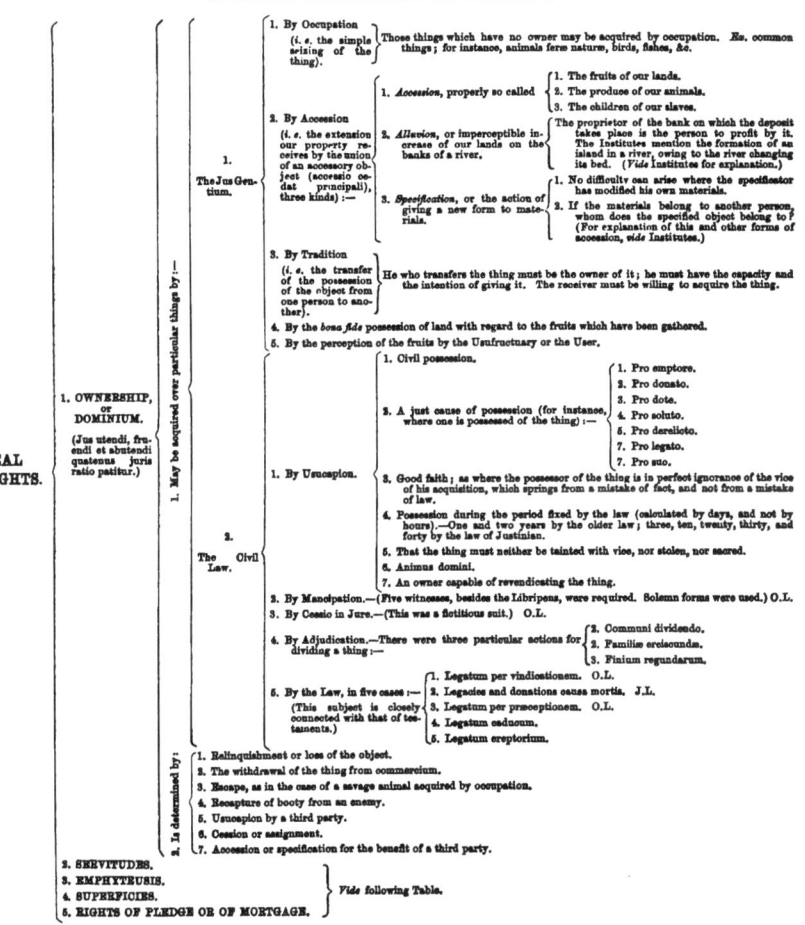

REAL RIGHTS.

1. OWNERSHIP, or DOMINIUM. (Jus utendi, fruendi et abutendi quatenus juris ratio patitur.)

1. May be acquired over particular things by :—

1. The Jus Gentium.

1. By Occupation (*i. e.* the simple seizing of the thing). — Those things which have no owner may be acquired by occupation. *Ex.* common things; for instance, animals feræ naturæ, birds, fishes, &c.

2. By Accession (*i. e.* the extension our property receives by the union, of an accessory object (accessio cedat principali), three kinds) :—

1. *Accession*, properly so called
  1. The fruits of our lands.
  2. The produce of our animals.
  3. The children of our slaves.

2. *Alluvion*, or imperceptible increase of our lands on the banks of a river. — The proprietor of the bank on which the deposit takes place is the person to profit by it. The Institutes mention the formation of an island in a river, owing to the river changing its bed. (*Vide* Institutes for explanation.)

3. *Specification*, or the action of giving a new form to materials.
  1. No difficulty can arise where the specificator has modified his own materials.
  2. If the materials belong to another person, whom does the specified object belong to? (For explanation of this and other forms of accession, *vide* Institutes.)

3. By Tradition (*i. e.* the transfer of the possession of the object from one person to another). — He who transfers the thing must be the owner of it; he must have the capacity and the intention of giving it. The receiver must be willing to acquire the thing.

4. By the *bona fide* possession of land with regard to the fruits which have been gathered.

5. By the perception of the fruits by the Usufructuary or the User.

2. The Civil Law.

1. By Usucapion.
  1. Civil possession.
  2. A just cause of possession (for instance, where one is possessed of the thing) :—
    1. Pro emptore.
    2. Pro donato.
    3. Pro dote.
    4. Pro soluto.
    5. Pro derelicto.
    6. Pro legato.
    7. Pro suo.
  3. Good faith; as where the possessor of the thing is in perfect ignorance of the vice of his acquisition, which springs from a mistake of fact, and not from a mistake of law.
  4. Possession during the period fixed by the law (calculated by days, and not by hours).—One and two years by the older law; three, ten, twenty, thirty, and forty by the law of Justinian.
  5. That the thing must neither be tainted with vice, nor stolen, nor sacred.
  6. Animus domini.
  7. An owner capable of revendicating the thing.

2. By Mancipation.—(Five witnesses, besides the Libripens, were required. Solemn forms were used.) O.L.

3. By Cessio in Jure.—(This was a fictitious suit.) O.L.

4. By Adjudication.—There were three particular actions for dividing a thing :—
  1. Communi dividendo.
  2. Familiæ erciscundæ.
  3. Finium regundarum.

5. By the Law, in five cases :— (This subject is closely connected with that of testaments.)
  1. Legatum per vindicationem. O.L.
  2. Legacies and donations causa mortis. J.L.
  3. Legatum per præceptionem. O.L.
  4. Legatum caducum.
  5. Legatum ereptorium.

2. Is determined by :
1. Relinquishment or loss of the object.
2. The withdrawal of the thing from commercium.
3. Escape, as in the case of a savage animal acquired by occupation.
4. Recapture of booty from an enemy.
5. Usucapion by a third party.
6. Cession or assignment.
7. Accession or specification for the benefit of a third party.

2. SERVITUDES.
3. EMPHYTEUSIS.
4. SUPERFICIES.
5. RIGHTS OF PLEDGE OR OF MORTGAGE.
} *Vide* following Table.

8

BOOK II.—TABLE VII.

Tɪᴛ. III.—De Servitutibus.   Tɪᴛ. IV.—De Usufructu.   Tɪᴛ. V.—De Usu et Habitatione.

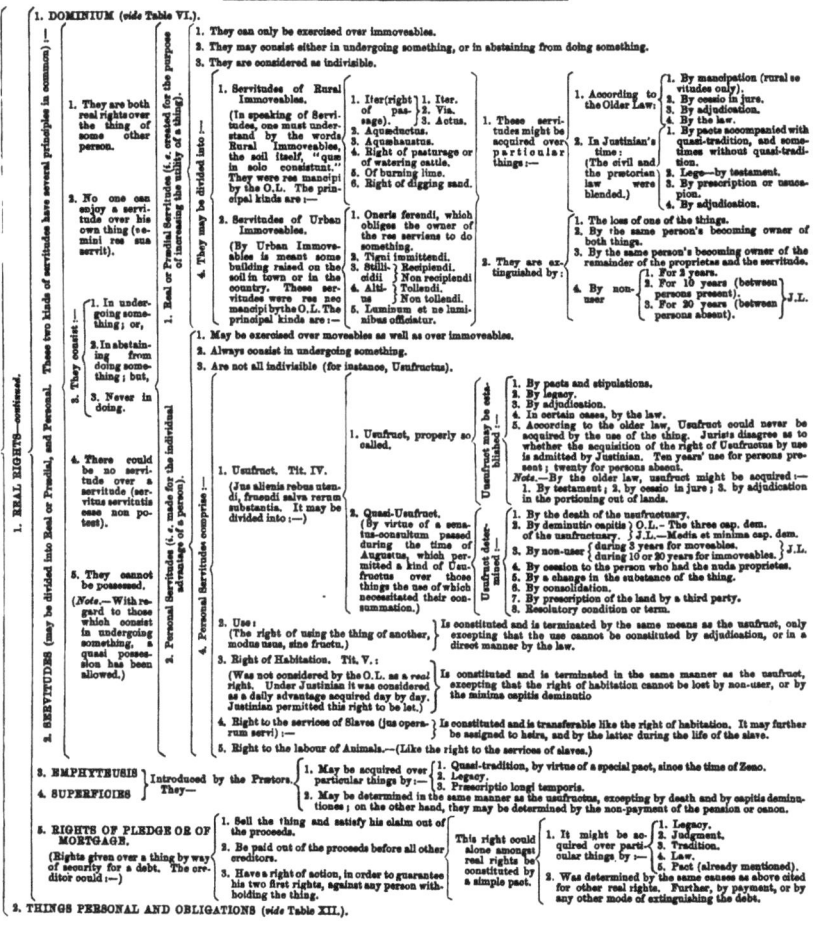

BOOK II.—TABLE VIII.

Tit. VII.—De Donationibus.   Tit. VIII.—Quibus alienare licet, vel non.

Tit. IX.—Per quas Personas cuique acquiritur.

OF DONATIONS.

(A " Donatio " is a translation of property made out of generosity (dono datio). Property can only be acquired by donation over a particular thing, in cases of donatio " mortis causâ."— There are two kinds of donations :)

TIT. VII.

1. DONATION " MORTIS CAUSÂ."

(Which is conditional on the decease of the donor, or even of a third person ; it is revocable at the will of the donor. Donations " causâ mortis " may be either *suspensive* or *resolutory*. A donation " mortis causâ."—)

1. Resembles a Legacy—

1. In that it is revocable.
2. In that it may only be made or received by those who can make, or by those who can receive, a legacy.
3. In that it has to be paid out of the real effects.
4. In that the heir, by virtue of the " lex Falcidia," can have the legacies reduced.
5. In that it is capable of receiving an increase.
6. In that it transfers the property by itself on the death of the donor.

2. Differs from a Legacy—

1. In that it requires to be accepted by the donee during the donor's lifetime.
2. In that it becomes realised by the simple fact of the donor's death.
3. In that regard is had to the capacity to receive of the person to whom the gift is made only at the time of the death, and not, as in the case of legacies, also at the time of the disposition.
4. In that it can transfer a resolutory property to the donee during the lifetime of the donor, which never happens in the case of legacies.

2. DONATION " INTER VIVOS."

(Without "mortis causâ.")

The giver disposes at once and irrevocably of that which forms the object of his liberality. The distinctive feature of donations " inter vivos" is the irrevocability of the gift, excepting in the case of ingratitude on the part of the donee, and in the single case of a child's being unexpectedly born to a " patronus " who had given away, of his property away to his " libertus."

Donations " ante nuptias " were, however, always conditional. *Under Justinian,* this donation was called " propter nuptias," it was made before the marriage, for all gifts between husband and wife were prohibited by the law. (*Vide* Table I.—Unwritten Law.)

Since Justinian's time, donations may be made—

1. Verbis.
2. Literis.
3. Consensu.
4. Sine insinuatione in some cases, and also in the case of the gift of a sum under 500 solidi.

Of those who may, and of those who may not, alienate.

TIT. VIII.

1. OF THOSE PERSONS WHO, ALTHOUGH OWNERS, MAY NOT ALIENATE.

1. THE HUSBAND—

1. *Before Justinian's time,* could not alienate immoveables situated in Italy, forming part of his wife's dowry, without the consent of the latter. Further, he could not mortgage them, even with her consent.
2. *Since Justinian's time,* he can neither sell nor subject them to a hypotheca, even with his wife's consent.

2. THE PUPIL—   Could not alienate anything without his tutor's permission. (*Vide* the Institutes as to different cases relating to pupils.)

2. PERSONS WHO, WITHOUT BEING OWNERS, MAY ALIENATE.

1. THE CREDITOR may sell the thing given him as a pledge.
2. TUTORS and CURATORS may, with the magistrate's permission, alienate certain of the pupil's effects.

Through whom we may acquire.

TIT. IX.

1. BY OURSELVES.

2. BY OUR FILIIFAMILIAS.

But we may not acquire their " castrense," " quasicastrense," or " adventitium peculiums." (The Peculium consists in a certain amount of property distinct from the patrimony held in common.) There were several kinds of Peculium, viz. :—

1. *Castrense* ...... Everything acquired by the son in setting out upon, or acquired during, military service.
2. *Quasi-Castrense* ... Things which the filiusfamilias receives from the munificence of the prince in the exercise of certain civil functions.
3. *Adventitium* ... All things acquired by the son, but which do not proceed from the father.
4. *Profectitium* Things which come to the son as part of his father's property. The father had the usufruct over this peculium.

3. BY SLAVES.

The property acquired by the slave of several masters is divided in proportion to the rights each master has over him. As to those slaves over whom we have the right of usufruct, we may acquire through them all those things which they obtain by their industry.

4. BY WOMEN IN MANU MARITI.

5. BY FREE MEN IN MANCIPIO.

6. BY FREE MEN, whom we possess bona fide as slaves.

7. THE SLAVES OF OTHERS who are bona fide in our possession.

8. THE SLAVES OF OTHERS, but of whom we have only the user.

BOOK II.—TABLE IX.

Tit. X.—De Testamentis Ordinandis.   Tit. XI.—De Militari Testamento.

Tit. XII.—Quibus non est permissum facere Testamentum.   Tit. XIII.—De Exheredatione Liberorum.

Tit. XIV.—De Heredibus Instituendis.   Tit. XV.—De Vulgari Substitutione.   Tit. XVI.—De Pupillari Substitutione.

Tit. XVII.—Quibus Modis Testamenta infirmantur.   Tit. XVIII.—De Inofficioso Testamento.

Tit. XIX.—De Heredum Qualitate et Differentia.

TESTAMENTARY SUCCESSION.

(A Testament is "voluntatis nostræ justa sententia de eo quod quis post mortem suam fieri velit." It is necessary to observe in the making of a will—)

1. FACTIO TESTA-MENTIS. (Which comprises the power of making a will and that of receiving or securing for one's self, or for some other person, by the will of another. Had not this power:—)

1. Those who were not fathers of families. O.L.
2. Filii-familiarum with regard to the "castrense peculium," before the times of the Emperors Augustus, Nerva, and Trajan.
3. Filii-familiarum with regard to the "quasi-castrense peculium" before the days of Justinian.
4. Madmen, persons under the age of puberty, prodigals, deaf and dumb persons, though they be "sui juris"; in a word, all those who were incapable of making a will.
5. Roman citizens captives in the power of the enemy, although they subsequently return.
6. Slaves, strangers (peregrini), &c.

2. THE DIFFERENT KINDS OF TESTAMENT (these were):—

1. Calatis comitiis et in procinctu — The former will can be made at two periods in the year in an assembly of the "comitia curiata." Testaments "in procincta" are made in the presence of the army equipped and under arms (procinctus est expeditus et armatus exercitus).

2. Per Æs et Libram, O.L., by which— The whole of the patrimony (res mancipi) was sold by the testator with the formalities of mancipation to a buyer, who in the inception was the future inheritor himself, but who, in later times, was a third party, intervening as a pure matter of form only. The usufruct was reserved to the testator. The formal declaration of his wishes made by the testator was called "nuncupatio." The necessary parties to a will of this kind were—
   1. The testator.
   2. Five witnesses. (Roman citizens who had attained the age of puberty.)
   3. A Libripens.
   4. The Emptor-familiæ.

3. Prætorian Testament. Recognised by the Prætor. It is made by the testator without the assistance of the "Libripens" and the "Emptor-familiæ," but in the presence of seven witnesses, who each had to affix his seal. In the beginning, the Prætor did not give the inheritance properly so called, but only the "bonorum possessio."

4. Testamentum tripertitum. (Thus named because it owed its origin to three different legislations. J.L. Three conditions are necessary:—)
   1. Uno contextu; all the formalities must be accomplished immediately, and without interruption.
   2. Seven witnesses are required, to whom the testator hands over the will, which is written either by himself or by some other person; in the latter case it requires to be subscribed by the writer. Eight witnesses are necessary if the testator does not know how to write.
   3. The signatures of the witnesses, called "subscriptiones," when the will is open. "Signicula," i. e. the seals, when the will is closed.

3. THE INSTITUTION OF HEIRS.

1. May be made heirs all those who have factio testamenti with the testator. With the exception of the cases enumerated above, all Romans, and their slaves for them, have "factio testamenti."

2. A testator may appoint one heir or several; but whether he appoint one or several, they must have the whole of the inheritance, for no one can die partly testate and partly intestate. The "hereditas" is called by the Romans "as," and was divided into twelve equal parts, called ounces—

2 ounces, or 1/6 made	1/6	called sextrans.
3	"	1/4	"	quatrans.
4	"	1/3	"	triens.
6	"	1/2	"	semis.
8	"	2/3	"	bes.
9	"	3/4	"	dodrans.
10	"	5/6	"	dextrans.
11	"	11/12	"	deunx.

3. The heir
   1. May be—
      1. Pure.
      2. Sub conditions.
   2. May not be—
      1. Pure.
      2. Sub conditions.
      3. Ex certo tempore.
      4. Ad certum tempus. An institution made from, or to, a certain period, was considered as unwritten (pro supervacuo). We must not confound it with an institution "sub conditione."

4. Instituted heirs are divided into:
   1. Necessarii.—Slaves instituted heirs by their masters, at whose death they became free, and necessarily heirs.
   2. Sui et necessarii.—Sui, because the filiifamiliae during the lifetime of their father are considered as proprietors of the family fortune; and necessarii, because by the Older Law they became heirs, even as the slaves.
   3. Extranei, or strangers.—Those who are not under the power of the testator.

4. EXHEREDATIO (or, the disinheriting of heirs).

1. May be made—
   1. Nominatim (by name).
   2. Collectively (inter cæteros).
2. May be disinherited.
   1. Living children.
   2. Posthumous children, properly so called.
   3. Postumi Velleiani.
   4. Quasi-postumi Velleiani.

5. SUBSTITUTION (Conditional on another institution of an heir, on which it depends.)

1. Ordinary Substitution.—Conditional institution in case those persons who are instituted heirs should refuse or should be incapacitated from accepting. The number of substitutions is unlimited.
2. Pupillary Substitution.—The son's testament made by the father, as accessory to his own.
3. Exemplary, or Quasi-Pupillary, Substitution.—Is that which allows ascendants to substitute other persons in the place of those who, being under the age of puberty and deprived of reason, should die without becoming sane.

6. INVALIDATION (A will may be invalidated when it is—)

1. Injustum, or non jure factum, i. e. invalid from the beginning.
2. Ruptum, i. e. originally valid but rendered ineffectual ....
   1. By the unexpected arrival or agnation of a suus heres, who would neither have been instituted heir nor legally disinherited.
   2. By the making of a subsequent testament capable of giving an heir to the testator.
   3. By a legal revocation of the will by the testator, without his making another in its stead.
3. Irritum, i. e. when the testator suffers a capitis deminutio.
4. Destitutum, i. e. abandoned, by no one entering on the inheritance.
5. Inofficiosum. — Recti quidem factum non autem ex officio pietatis. A testament may be attacked as inofficiosus—
   1. By the children (the ascendants; brothers and sisters in the order in which they would have been called to succeed had no will been made.
   2. The will ceases to be "inofficious" when the heir of the blood has received the portion secured to him by the law (Lex Falcidia). This share is increased by Justinian, and when the heir has not received the whole of his share, he is only entitled to claim the residue. The will cannot be attacked by the heir—
      1. When he has once given his assent to it.
      2. After the lapse of { 2 yrs. O.L. { 5 yrs. J.L.
      3. After the death of the heir of the blood.

The actions relating to succession are:—
   1. Hæreditatis petitio.
   2. Familiæ erciscundæ.
   3. Querela inofficiosi testamenti.

These actions are peculiar to testamentary successions. (For explanation, vide "Actions.")

BOOK II.—TABLE X.

Tɪᴛ. XX.—De Legatis.   Tɪᴛ. XXI.—De Ademptione et Translatione Legatorum.
Tɪᴛ. XXII.—De Lege Falcidia.   Tɪᴛ. XXIII.—De Fidei-commissariis Hereditatibus.
Tɪᴛ. XXIV.—De Singulis Rebus per Fidei-commissum Relictis.   Tɪᴛ. XXV.—De Codicillis.

LEGACIES.

Legatum est donatio quædam a defuncto relicta.

A legacy only confers the right of property of servitude, or of real rights, differing therein from the institution of an heir, which has for object the passing of the Juridical "Persona" of the deceased on to the person instituted heir.

A legacy is, in law, imposed by the testator on the intestate heir, thereby differing (before Justinian's time) from a fidei-commiss. Justinian amalgamated the two.

Legacies may be examined relatively—

1. To their different kinds.
  - 1. Per Vindicationem.
    - In which the testator says to the legatee,—"Capito," "sumito," or only "Do," "lego." The testator can only give in this way things over which he has the "dominium ex jure Quiritium," both at the time of his death and at the time of the making of his testament.
  - 2. Per Damnationem.
    - In which the testator says to the legatee, "Hæres meus, damnas esto dare, dato, facito," etc. (Ulp. tit. xxiv. 4, 4.)
    - All things susceptible of being left as legacies may be disposed of by this method.
  - 3. Sinendi modo.
    - In which the testator says to the legatee, "Hæres meus, damnas esto sinere Lucium Titium sumere illam rem sibique habere." (Gaius, ii. 209.)
    - The legatee can acquire the property in the thing by taking possession of the thing left to him.
  - 4. Per Præceptionem.
    - In which the testator tells the legatee to take the object beforehand.
    - *N.B.*—All the differences between these four classes have disappeared, after having been modified by the sen. cons. Neronianum, by the constitutions of Constantine II., Constantina, and Constans. Dissatisfied with the fusion of legacies, Justinian assimilated them to the "fidei-commissa," which owed their origin to a desire on the part of the Roman citizens to be generous towards persons with whom they had not "factio testamenti."—*Vide* Tit. XIII.
    - "Fidei-commissa" underwent the following modifications:—
      - 1. Before the sen. cons. "Trebellianum"; stipulations "emptæ et venditæ hereditatis."
      - 2. According to the sen. cons. Trebellianum; direct actions for and against the "fidei-commissarius."
      - 3. According to the sen. cons. Pegasianum; stipulations "partis et pro parte."
      - 4. Under Justinian; direct actions (sen. consulta Trebellianum and Pegasianum amalgamated). The usual forms of fidei-commissa are:—Peto—volo—rogo—mando—fidei tuo committo, etc. (Tit. XXIV.); and one may dispose by "fidei-commissa," not only of the same objects that one might have willed away according to the older law, "per damnationem," but, again, one may charge the fidei-commissaria to give a different thing from that which one might have received as a legacy or as a "fidei-commissa."

2. To their object.
  - 1. What may be the object of a legacy.
    - 1. Things, in their nature objects of commerce, corporeal or incorporeal, present or future.
    - 2. The property of another person; in which case the heir is obliged to repurchase it, and give it to the legatee.
    - 3. Property belonging to the testator, but which he believed to belong to some other person, etc. For examples *vide* Institutes.
  - 2. What may not be the object of a legacy.
    - 1. Things which are not, in their nature, objects of commerce.
    - 2. Things which already belong to the legatee, &c.—*Vide* Institutes.

3. To the persons to whom they may be made.
  - One can only bequeath to those with whom one has factio of testament. Justinian, however, allowed uncertain persons to be instituted legatees, and to receive legacies or fidei-commissa, but not the testamentary tutelage.

4. To the causes of their revocation and of their translation. Legacies may be revoked or transferred.—Tɪᴛ. XXI.
  - 1. By the simple will of the testator, expressly or tacitly pronounced.
  - 2. By the sale of the object, if the institution of the revocation accompanies the sale.
  - 3. By translation.
  - 4. If the legatee does not come forward to receive his legacy, &c.   *Note.*
    - The "Lex Falcidia" further forbids a testator to give away more than three-fourths of his property in legacies; consequently the heir may always possess, at the least, one-fourth of the property. This fourth goes by the name of the "Quarta Falcidia."

5. To their condition.
  - Conditio (Muciana cautio).

6. To the motive for which they are given.
  - Pœnæ nomine legatum—Needless disposition, O. L. valable under Justinian; but differing from an ordinary conditional legacy, in that the impossible or illegal condition is not supposed to be unwritten, but to annul the legacy.

7. To their mode.
  - Modus.

8. To the effect of:—
  - 1. Dies cedit (the right to the thing is fixed)—
    - At the death of the testator, if the legacy be "pure." The Lex Julia Poppæa retarded the "dies cedit" until the day when the testament was opened. Under Justinian the old law was in force. On the happening of the condition, if the legacy be conditional.
    - The principles of the "dies cedit" rule the losses, the augmentations, and the diminutions of the bequeathed objects.
  - 2. Dies venit (the thing may be demanded)—
    - 1. When the heir enters upon the inheritance.
    - 2. When the term has expired, if the legacy be given after a term.
    - 3. On the fulfilment of the condition, if the legacy be given on a condition.
    - The "dies cedit" exercises its influence over—
      - 1. The choice of the persons by whom the legacy may be acquired.
      - 2. The things which form the object of the legacy.
      - 3. The assignment of the right bequeathed.
      - 4. The loss or the preservation of the bequeathed right.
  - Regula Catoniana, according to which—
    - All legacies which would have been invalid if the testator had died immediately after making his will are invalid until such death; therefore, in order to ascertain the validity of a legacy, we must suppose that the testator died as soon as he had made his will.

OF CODICILS.

1. A codicil is an act by which a person expresses his last wishes, without employing, and with the intention of not employing the solemnity of a testament. Codicils were introduced by Lentulus.
2. Persons dying intestate may make codicils; but those who have the capacity of making a will, are alone capable of making them.
3. A "clausula codicillaris" was a clause inserted in a testament, providing that if the testament were invalid it should take effect as a codicils.

12

BOOK III.—TABLE XI.

Tit. I.—De Hereditatibus quæ ab Intestato deferuntur.   Tit. II.—De Legitima Agnatorum Successione.
Tit. III.—De Senatus-Consulto Tertulliano.   Tit. IV.—De Senatus-Consulto Orphitiano.
Tit. V.—De Successione Cognatorum.   Tit. VI.—De Gradibus Cognationis.   Tit. VII.—De Successione Libertorum.
Tit. VIII.—De Assignatione Libertorum.   Tit. IX.—De Bonorum Possessionibus.
Tit. X.—De Acquisitione per Arrogationem.   Tit. XI.—De Eo cui Libertatis Causa bona addicuntur.
Tit. XII.—De Successionibus sublatis, quæ fiebant per bonorum venditionem, et ex Senatus-Consulto Claudiano.

BOOK III.—TABLE XII.

Tit. XIII.—De Obligationibus.   Tit. XIV.—Quibus Modis Re contrahitur Obligatio.
Tit. XV.—De Verborum Obligatione.   Tit. XVI.—De Duobus Reis Stipulandi et Promittendi.
Tit. XVII.—De Stipulatione Servorum.   Tit. XVIII.—De Divisione Stipulationum.
Tit. XIX.—De Inutilibus Stipulationibus.   Tit. XX.—De Fidejussoribus.   Tit. XXI.—De Literarum Obligatione.
Tit. XXII.—De Consensu Obligatione.   Tit. XXIII.—De Emptione et Venditione.
Tit. XXIV.—De Locatione et Conductione.   Tit. XXV.—De Societate.   Tit. XXVI.—De Mandato.
Tit. XXVII.—De Obligationibus quasi ex Contractu.   Tit. XXVIII.—Per quas Personas nobis Obligatio adquiritur.
Tit. XXIX.—Quibus Modis Obligatio tollitur.

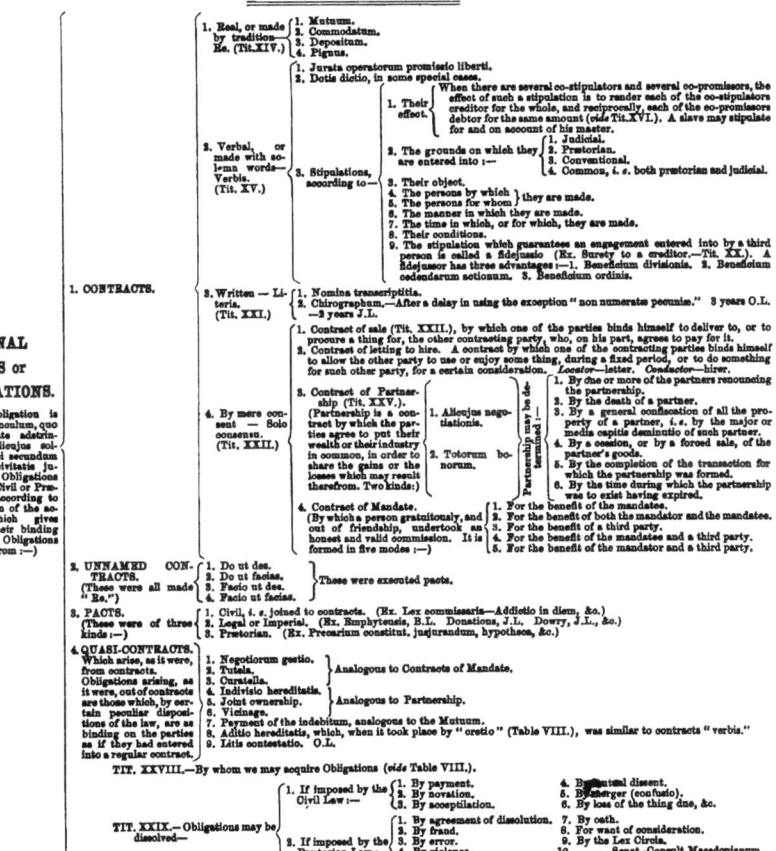

BOOK IV.—TABLE XIII.

Tit. I.—De Obligationibus quæ ex Delicto nascuntur.   Tit. II.—De Vi Bonorum raptorum.

Tit. III.—De Lege Aquilia.

Tit. IV.—De Injuriis.   Tit. V.—De Obligationibus quæ quasi ex Delicto nascuntur.

OBLIGATIONS, arising—

1. EX DELICTO. (Delicta were wrong and illegal acts, to procure reparation, for which the law provided a special action. Two kinds of delicta—)

2. PRIVATE. (Which give a right of action to certain particular persons only.)

1. PUBLIC, which may give a right of action to every citizen.

1. Furtum.

1. Manifestum, in which the penalty inflicted is payment of four times the value of the thing stolen.

2. Nec manifestum, in which the penalty inflicted is payment of double the value of the thing stolen.

The older law divided thefts into—

1. Furtum conceptum.
2. „ oblatum.
3. „ prohibitum.
4. „ non exhibitum.

These gave birth to different kinds of actions.

2. Raptum. Where a person forcibly takes a thing belonging to another. In this case there is a peculiar kind of action called "Vi Bonorum raptorum," by which, if brought within a year after the robbery, four times the value of the thing stolen may be recovered; but if brought after the expiration of a year, the single value of the thing can alone be recovered.

3. Damnum. (Punished by the Lex Aquilia. Tit. III.)

The first head of the Lex Aquilia treats of the wrongful (injuria) killing of the slave, or of the four-footed beast (pecudum numero) of another .... of Horses, Mules, Sheep, Swine, Goats, Oxen, &c. The wrongdoer was obliged to pay the greatest value of the thing during the preceding year.

The second head of the Lex Aquilia relates to adstipulators who have freed their debtors by acceptilation, and thus fraudulently extinguished the stipulator's claim against such debtors.

The third head of the Lex Aquilia relates to all wrongful injury caused by the destruction of things other than slaves, and those quadrupeds whose nature it is to feed in flocks and herds.

2. QUASI EX DELICTO.

1. Si judex litem suam fecerit.
2. Si dejectum effusum aliquid est.
3. Positum aut suspensum habet.
4. Quasi delictum. Where damage or loss, through theft, occurs in a ship, inn, or stable.

BOOK IV.—TABLE XIII.

Tit. VI.—De Actionibus.   Tit. VII.—Quod cum eo contractum est qui in aliena potestate est.
Tit. VIII.—De Noxalibus Actionibus.   Tit. IX.—Si quadrupes pauperiem fecisse dicatur.
Tit. X.—De iis per quos agere possumus.   Tit. XI.—De Satisdationibus.
Tit. XII.—De Perpetuis et Temporalibus Actionibus, et quæ ad heredes et in heredes transeunt.

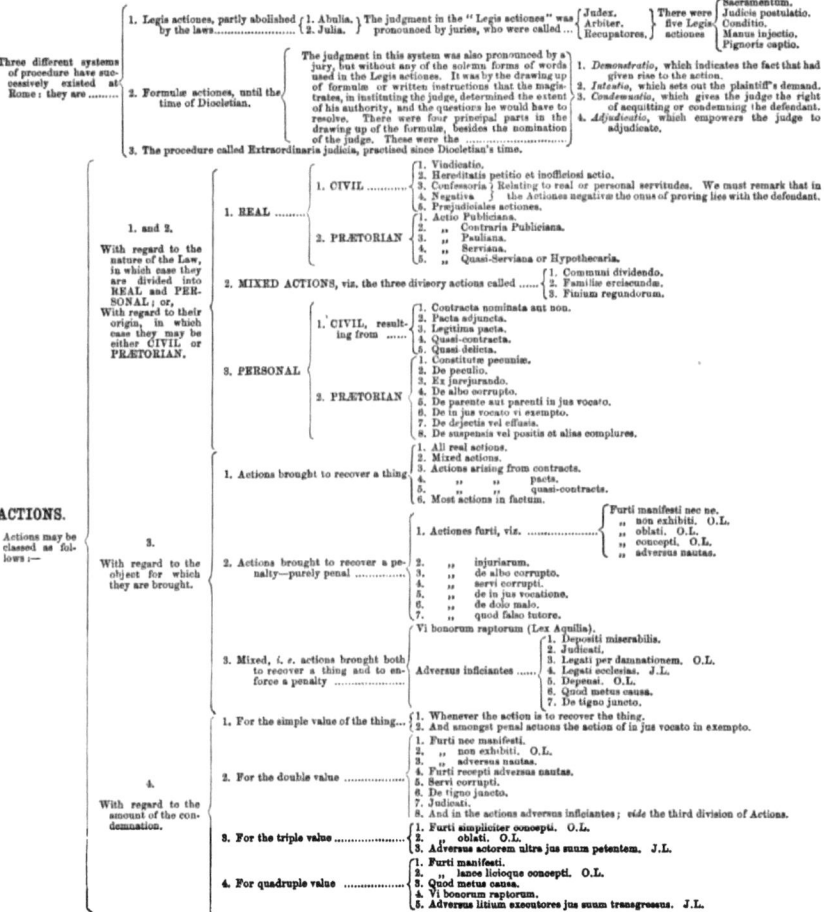

Three different systems of procedure have been successively existed at Rome: they are

1. Legis actiones, partly abolished by the laws ....

   1. Abulia.   2. Julia. } The judgment in the "Legis actiones" was pronounced by juries, who were called ... { Judex. Arbiter. Recuperatores. } There were five Legis actiones { Sacramentum. Judicis postulatio. Conditio. Manus injectio. Pignoris captio.

2. Formulæ actiones, until the time of Diocletian.

The judgment in this system was also pronounced by a jury, but without any of the solemn forms of words used in the Legis actiones. It was by the drawing up of formulæ or written instructions that the magistrates, in instituting the judge, determined the extent of his authority, and the questions he would have to resolve. There were four principal parts in the drawing up of the formulæ, besides the nomination of the judge. These were the—

1. *Demonstratio*, which indicates the fact that had given rise to the action.
2. *Intentio*, which sets out the plaintiff's demand.
3. *Condemnatio*, which gives the judge the right of acquitting or condemning the defendant.
4. *Adjudicatio*, which empowers the judge to adjudicate.

3. The procedure called Extraordinaria judicia, practised since Diocletian's time.

ACTIONS.

Actions may be classed as follows:—

1. and 2. With regard to the nature of the Law, in which case they are divided into REAL and PERSONAL; or, With regard to their origin, in which case they may be either CIVIL or PRÆTORIAN.

1. REAL

  1. CIVIL ....
1. Vindicatio.
2. Hereditatis petitio et inofficiosi actio.
3. Confessoria } Relating to real or personal servitudes. We must remark that in the Actiones negativæ the onus of proving lies with the defendant.
4. Negativa
5. Prejudiciales actiones.

  2. PRÆTORIAN
1. Actio Publiciana.
2. „ Contraria Publiciana.
3. „ Pauliana.
4. „ Serviana.
5. „ Quasi-Serviana or Hypothecaria.

2. MIXED ACTIONS, viz. the three divisory actions called ......
1. Communi dividendo.
2. Familiæ erciscundæ.
3. Finium regundorum.

3. PERSONAL

  1. CIVIL, resulting from ......
1. Contracta nominata aut non.
2. Pacta adjuncta.
3. Legitima pacta.
4. Quasi-contracta.
5. Quasi delicta.

  2. PRÆTORIAN
1. Constitutæ pecuniæ.
2. De peculio.
3. Ex jurejurando.
4. De albo corrupto.
5. De parente aut parenti in jus vocato.
6. De in jus vocato vi exempto.
7. De dejectis vel effusis.
8. De suspensis vel positis et aliis compluribus.

3. With regard to the object for which they are brought.

1. Actions brought to recover a thing
1. All real actions.
2. Mixed actions.
3. Actions arising from contracts.
4. „ „ pacts.
5. „ „ quasi-contracts.
6. Most actions in factum.

2. Actions brought to recover a penalty—purely penal
1. Actiones furti, viz. ......
Furti manifesti nec ne.
„ non exhibiti. O.L.
„ oblati. O.L.
„ concepti. O.L.
„ adversus nautas.
2. „ injuriarum.
3. „ de albo corrupto.
4. „ servi corrupti.
5. „ de in jus vocatione.
6. „ de dolo malo.
7. „ quod falso tutore.
Vi bonorum raptorum (Lex Aquilia).

3. Mixed, i. e. actions brought both to recover a thing and to enforce a penalty
Adversus inficiantes ......
1. Depositi miserabilis.
2. Judicati.
3. Legati per damnationem. O.L.
4. Legati ecclesiæ. J.L.
5. Depensi. O.L.
6. Quod metus causa.
7. De tigno juncto.

4. With regard to the amount of the condemnation.

1. For the simple value of the thing....
1. Whenever the action is to recover the thing.
2. And amongst penal actions the action of in jus vocato in exempto.

2. For the double value
1. Furti nec manifesti.
2. „ non exhibiti. O.L.
3. „ adversus nautas.
4. Furti recepti adversus nautas.
5. Servi corrupti.
6. De tigno juncto.
7. Judicati.
8. And in the actions adversus inficiantes; vide the third division of Actions.

3. For the triple value
1. Furti simpliciter concepti. O.L.
2. „ oblati. O.L.
3. Adversus actorem ultra jus suum petentem. J.L.

4. For quadruple value
1. Furti manifesti.
2. „ lance licioque concepti. O.L.
3. Quod metus causa.
4. Vi bonorum raptorum.
5. Adversus litium executores jus suum transgressos. J.L.

BOOK IV.—TABLE XIV (continued).

ACTIONS—continued.

5. With regard to the powers given to the judge.

1. Bonæ Fidei Actions. (Which give the judge the power of ruling, not according to the rigour of the civil law, but according to equity.)

1. Familiæ erciscundæ.	7. Pigneratitia.	13. Negotiorum gestorum.
2. Communi dividundo.	8. Empti venditi.	14. Tutelæ.
3. Præscriptis verbis.	9. Locati conducti.	15. Negotiorum gestorum utilis curæ.
4. Petitio hereditatis. J.L.	10. Emphyteuticaria.	16. Fiduciæ. O.L.
5. Commodati.	11. Pro socio.	17. Rei uxoriæ. O.L.
6. Depositi.	12. Mandati.	18. Ex stipulatu de dote. J.L.

2. Stricti Juris. (In which the judge is obliged to adhere strictly to the principles of the civil law.)

1. Ex stipulatu.	6. Receptitia. O.L.	11. Condictio ex lege.
2. Ex mutuo.	7. Judicati.	12. Condictio indebiti.
3. Ex dictione dotis. O.L.	8. Legis Aquiliæ.	13. Condictio sine causa data.
4. Ex operarum promissione.	9. Depensi.	14. Condictio ob turpem causam.
5. Ex testamento.	10. Condictio certi ex literis.	15. Condictio furtiva.

3. Arbitrary. (In which the judge may determine what satisfaction the defendant must give to the plaintiff, and acquits the former when he has given the prescribed satisfaction.)

1. Real.
  1. Civil.
  2. Prætorian.

2. Personal.
  1. Quod metus causa.
  2. De dolo malo.
  3. De eo quod certo loco.
  4. Ad exhibendum.
  5. Actions arising from interdicts { 1. Restitutory. 2. Exhibitory. }

3. Mixed. Finium regundorum.

6. With regard to the totality of what is due.

Actions in which sometimes the whole, sometimes less than the whole, of what is due is obtained. Ex. Action "de Peculio," in which the debtor may enjoy the privilege called "beneficium competentiæ."

7. With regard to contracts made by persons "alieni juris." (Tit. VII.)

1. Direct actions, i. e. brought against a person bound by some act of his own.

2. Indirect actions, i. e. those which do not result from the act of the person against whom they are brought. The Prætors allowed six indirect actions against the Paterfamilias which result from contracts entered into with his sons and with his slaves. They are :—
  1. Quod jussu.
  2. Exercitoria.
  3. Institoria.
  4. Tributoria.
  5. De peculio.
  6. De in rem verso.

8. Noxal actions.
1. Arising from the wrongful act of a Filiusfamilias, or of a slave.
2. Arising from damage done by animals (action de pauperie. Tit. IX.).

9. With regard to their duration.
1. Perpetual. { Civil actions before the latter empire, i. e. actions derived from the law, from a senatus-consultum, from imperial constitutions, or from any other source of the civil law.
2. Temporary. Usually lasting but one year. Temporary actions were actions derived from a prætorian edict.
3. Treuntinary. { In the time of Justinian the term perpetual no longer had its former meaning ; it was applied to trentinary actions, or actions which could not be brought after a lapse of thirty, and in some cases of forty, years.

10. With regard to their transmission to heirs.
1. Transmissible to and against heirs.—All actions excepting those that are not transmissible.
2. Not transmissible
  1. To heirs ...... { 1. When they result from adstipulations. 2. Action of "Injuriarum." }
  2. Against heirs { 1. Arising from "sponsio." 2. Penal and mixed actions. }

11th Division.
1. Legitima Judicia. { 1. Place : in the city of Rome, or within the first milestone round it. 2. Litigants : Roman citizens. 3. Tried by a single Roman judge. }
2. Judicia Imperio continentia.—All the other "judicia."

12th Division.
1. In Jus. { 1. All civil actions. 2. Fictitious prætorian actions. }
2. In Factum.—All other prætorian actions.

13th Division.
1. Directæ, i. e. established for the enforcement of some particular right.
2. Utiles, i. e. extended to an unforeseen but analogous case.

14th Division.
1. Direct, quæ suæ vi ac potestate valent.
2. Fictitious.
  1. Actio Publiciana, directa et contraria.
  2. " Pauliana et Flaviana.
  3. " Rectiliana (emptori bonorum).
  4. " Serviani (possessori bonorum).
  5. A few "actiones utiles."

BY WHOM WE MAY BE REPRESENTED IN AN ACTION—OF CAUTIO AND OF SATISDATIO.

1. An action may be brought by any person whose rights have been assailed. He may be represented in such action by the following persons, who may bring such action in their own proper names :— (Vide Tit. X.)

1. A Tutor. According to the Older Law, at the time of the "Legis Actiones," no person could represent another, excepting in three cases :— { 1. Pro populo. 2. Pro libertate. 3. Pro tutela. }

2. A Curator. Under the system of "Formulæ," the representation of litigants became more general, and the following persons were permitted to represent others :— { 1. Loquitores. 2. Procuratores. 3. Defensores. 4. Tutores. 5. Curatores. 6. Cognitores. }

3. A Procurator. Under the last period of the Roman legal system, the period of "Extraordinaria Judicia," the "Cognitores" were done away with, and the custom of representation became still more general.

2. The Litigants were bound to give security to each other. (Vide Tit. XI.)

1. In Real Actions.
  1. On the Plaintiff's side :—Cautio de rato (if he were represented by a procurator).
  2. On the Defendant's side :—Cautio—
    1. De dolo.
    2. De persequendo servo, restituendo pretio.
    3. Rem pupilli salvam fore. O.L.
    4. Judicatum solvi (when he pleaded in person). O.L.
    5. Judicatum solvi (when he was represented by a procurator).

    The Cautio Judicatum solvi originally secured three objects :
    { De re judicata. De re defendenda. De dolo malo. }
    At a later period two objects only were secured by it :—
    { De sua tantum persona. Pro litis æstimatione }

2. In Personal Actions.
  1. On the Plaintiff's side :—Cautio de rato (if he were represented by a procurator).
  2. On the Defendant's side :—
    1. Cautio judicatum solvi. O.L.
      In the action judicati.
      { " " depensi. " " de moribus mulieris. " " against him "qui decoxerat." " " against a suspected heir. }
    2. Cautio judicatum solvi :—By the procurator "absentis."
    3. Cautio de rato :—By the "defensor."

BOOK IV.—TABLE XV.

Tɪᴛ. XIII.—De Exceptionibus.   Tɪᴛ. XIV.—De Replicationibus.   Tɪᴛ. XV.—De Interdictis.

Tɪᴛ. XVI.—De Pœna temere litigantium.

Tɪᴛ. XVII.—De Officio Judicis.   Tɪᴛ. XVIII.—De publicis Judiciis.

TIT. XIII. XIV.

OF THE MEANS OF DE-FENDING AN ACTION.

1. **EXCEPTIONS**
Were equitable restrictions introduced by the Prætor to oppose to the order to condemn, given to the judge in the "Intentio." These were:—
  1. Perpetual
    { 1. Doli.
    { 2. Pacti conventi.
  2. Peremptory .... Non numeratæ pecuniæ. (These were also temporary.)
  3. Temporary or Dilatory
    1. By reason of time ...
      { 1. Nisi bonus cesserit.
      { 2. Cognitoriæ.
      { 3. Pacti ad tempus.
      { 4. Rei residuæ. } O.L.
      { 5. Litis dividuæ.
      { 6. Procuratoriæ.
      { 7. In id quod facere potest.
    2. By reason of the person... Procuratoriæ.
  4. In rem.
  5. In personam.
  6. In jus { doli mali.
           { quod metus causa.
  7. In factum (too numerous to be cited).

2. **REPLICATIONS......** Are allegations added to the formulæ for the purpose of resolving and destroying the effect of an exception : they are exceptions put forward against an exception. Duplicatio is a double replication, &c.

TIT. XV.

OF INTERDICTS.

(Interdicts were certain formulæ by which the Prætor ordered or forbade something to be done. They were only made in special cases. They may be divided into :—)

1. **PROHIBITORY ......**
  1. Uti possidetis.
  2. Utrubi.
  3. De mortuo inferendo.
  4. De itinere actuque privato.
  5. De aqua æstiva.
  6. De aqua quotidiana.
  7. De fonte.
  8. De rivis.
  9. De cloacis.
  10. De migrando.
  11. De arboribus cædendis.
  12. De quis novi nuntiatione.

2. **RESTITUTORY ......**
  1. Quorum bonorum.
  2. Quod legatorum.
  3. Salvianum.
  4. Unde vi.
  5. Quod vi aut clam.
  6. De precario.
  7. Quod fraudandi causa.

3. **EXHIBITORY ....**
  1. De homine libero exhibendo.
  2. De liberis exhibendis.
  3. De eo cujus libertate agitur.
  4. De tabulis exhibendis.
  5. De liberto exhibendo.

4. **WITH REGARD TO POSSESSION ONLY ....**
  1. Adipiscendæ possessionis
    1. Quorum bonorum.
    2. Quod legatorum.
    3. Salvianum.
    4. Possessorium.
    5. Sectorium.
  2. Retinendæ possessionis ....
    1. Uti possidetis.
    2. Utrubi.
    3. De superficiebus.
    4. De rivis.
    5. De fonte.
    6. De cloacis.
    7. De aqua æstiva.
    8. De aqua quotidiana.
    9. De itinere actuque privato.
  3. Recuperandæ possessionis
    1. Unde vi.
    2. De clandestina possessione.
    3. De precario.
  4. Duplicia
    1. Quem fundum.
    2. Quam hereditatem.
    3. Quem usumfructum.

5. **SIMPLE ....** } These afford but little interest.
6. **DOUBLE ....** }

TIT. XVI. and TIT. XVII.

OF THE OFFICE OF THE JUDGE.

(A judge must judge according to the Senatus-consulta, the constitution, and customary usage. He is also empowered to punish those persons who engage recklessly in lawsuits.)

1. **AGAINST THE CLAIMANT ......**
  1. Judicium calumniæ.
  2.   „   contrarium.
  3. Loss of the action. O.L. } request for } Re
  4. Various punishments. J.L. }   delay.   { Tempore.
                                              { Loco.
                                              { Causa.
  5. Jusjurandum calumniæ.
  6. Restipulatio.

2. **AGAINST THE DE-FENDANT ....**
  1. Sponsio.
  2. Jusjurandum calumniæ.
  3. Infamy.
  4. Condemnation to pay double.

TIT. XVIII.

PUBLIC PROSECUTIONS

(Are criminal charges which the law allows any citizen to institute against any one who has been guilty of a crime, in order that the punishment attached by the law to such crime may be inflicted. Public prosecutions may be :—)

1. **CAPITAL ....**
  1. Lex Julia majestatis. (Crime of high treason.)
  2. „   de adulteria.
  3. „   Cornelia de sicariis. (Assassins.)
  4. „   Pompeia de paricidiis. (Parricides.)
  5. „   Cornelia de falsis. (Forgery.)
  6. „   Julia de vi publica seu privata. (Violence, with or without arms.)

2. **NOT CAPITAL ......**
  7. „   de peculatu. (Robbers of public money.)
  8. „   Fabia de plagiariis. (Keeping a free man in irons, or selling him as a slave.)
  9. „   Julia de ambitu. (Illegal methods of seeking offices.)
  10. „   „ repetundarum. (Bribery.)
  11. „   de annona. (Combinations to heighten the price of provisions.)
  12. „   de residuis. (Rendering incomplete account of, or misapplying, public monies.)

(The laws authorizing public prosecutions are)

THE END.